KT-417-494

BBC CHILDREN'S BOOKS
UK | USA | Canada | Ireland | Australia
India | New Zealand | South Africa

BBC Children's Books are published by Puffin Books,
part of the Penguin Random House group of companies whose
addresses can be found at global.penguinrandomhouse.com.

www.penguin.co.uk
www.puffin.co.uk
www.ladybird.co.uk

Penguin Random House UK

First published 2016
001

Written by Paul Lang
Illustrations: page 13 by James Newman Gray,
pages 38-41 by Arpad Olbey
Comic illustrations by John Ross, comic colours by James Offredi
pages 23-28 and 45-50

Printed in Italy

A CIP catalogue record for this book
is available from the British Library

ISBN: 978-1-405-92649-2

All correspondence to:
BBC Children's Books
Penguin Random House Children's
80 Strand, London, WC2R 0RL

CONTENTS

FIND THE SONIC SUNGLASSES

The Doctor loves wearing his shades – but he's dropped ten pairs of them throughout time and space!

Write down the page number of each pair of sunglasses you spot.

THE COMPLETE HISTORY OF THE DOCTOR

By me, the Doctor!
With help from ME, Missy!

You know the basics – Time Lord, TARDIS, rattling around the universe, fighting monsters, having adventures, blah, blah, blah. But have you heard the whole story of my life?

I'd nip to the loo now, if I were you – this might take a while.

My story starts as all the best ones do – with the theft of a time machine. I was either bored or terrified of life on my own planet, depending on who's asking. So I got out, and took my granddaughter, Susan, with me.

Susan! I'd forgotten all about her. Oh, she was ANNOYING. Forever screaming and falling over!

Oi! Susan's a lovely girl. Much nicer than you . . . Oh, never mind. Where were we?

We stopped off on Earth in 1963, and Susan went to Coal Hill School. (Interesting place – must remember to keep an eye on it.) Two teachers thought it was weird that we were living in a police box and, despite it being none of their business, came poking around. So, obviously, I decided the best thing to do was to kidnap them.

You were so much more UNPREDICTABLE in those days! I liked that.

One of the first places the four of us visited was Skaro – the planet of the Daleks! What are the odds? I could probably work them out if I wasn't busy writing this. I didn't know it then, but I would end up fighting them all through time, space and beyond.

You've blown up that planet at least twice that I know of. Are you surprised they hate you?

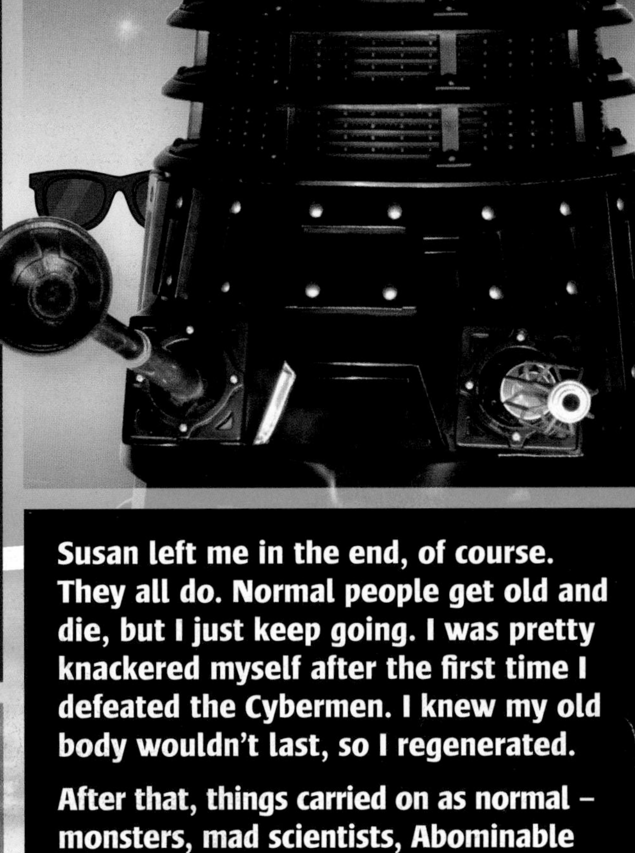

Susan left me in the end, of course. They all do. Normal people get old and die, but I just keep going. I was pretty knackered myself after the first time I defeated the Cybermen. I knew my old body wouldn't last, so I regenerated.

After that, things carried on as normal – monsters, mad scientists, Abominable Snowmen, you know the sort of thing.

Eventually I got into a spot of bother that I couldn't handle alone, so I had to call on the Time Lords. BIG. MISTAKE. They put me on trial for breaking their stupid rules, changed my face again and stranded me on Earth.

Which is where I came in! Marvellous.

The first thing I had to do was get a job. Me! A job!

Luckily, my old pals at UNIT – the Unified Intelligence Task Force – were looking for someone to do tricky science stuff. That kept me busy for a few years, and I even managed to sneak off and visit the occasional planet.

Eventually, I did the Time Lords a favour and they let me loose again – so I was back in business, having amazing adventures with amazing friends. I even got a robot dog! Why don't I have a robot dog now? I should get a robot dog . . .

But there were dark times to come.

You're telling me. Didn't I dress up as a scarecrow and stand in a field for some reason around this time? What WAS I thinking?

Shush, you – this is serious. Eventually, the Daleks and Time Lords started a war that neither could ever win. I tried not to get involved, but in the end, I had no choice. Doctor no more – I became a warrior. I used a terrible weapon and everyone burned in an instant – all the Daleks and all the Time Lords.

The Brigadier – my boss at UNIT, and Kate Stewart's dad.

I had to start from scratch as the Doctor again. But I could never forget what I'd done – especially when I found out the Daleks had survived.

And me! I survived too! It's all Daleks, Daleks, Daleks with you, isn't it?

Life seemed to get extra complicated around the time I met Amy Pond. First we were stalked by a giant crack in the universe which turned out to be erasing time itself. I had to reboot the universe to fix things. Then Amy had a baby, who was kidnapped and grew up to be River Song, who I married, despite technically being dead at the time.

SHHH! SPOILERS, SWEETIE! I EXPLAIN ALL THIS ON PAGE 30 . . .

Oh, not you as well! Whose story IS this?

Anyway, I then met Clara Oswald – that wonderful, impossible girl. Then I met her again. Then I met her AGAIN! I told you she was impossible. She was shattered into a million pieces and scattered through my timeline, so there was a version of her there to help me whenever I needed it. She was even there on Gallifrey when I first stole the TARDIS!

She led me to a face I thought I'd never see again: my own, the version I used when I fought in the Time War. With a bit of help from some other Doctors – the skinny fella and the one with the chin – they managed to undo what I'd done, meaning Gallifrey was just hidden, not destroyed. All I had to do was find it again.

I knew it was hidden all along. Just saying.

That was one quest I wouldn't care to repeat! Have you ever spent four and a half billion years slowly chipping away at a wall of solid diamond? No, you probably haven't. Well, I wouldn't recommend it.

Which brings us up to the present. Or is it the past? Or the future? Clara's gone now, just like all the others. I don't even remember her face – not properly, anyway. But I'll never forget the most important thing she told me: to be a Doctor. Never cruel or cowardly. Never giving up, never giving in.

Oh, pass the sick bucket!

MY REGENERATIONS

When my body gets damaged, I get a brand-new one. Just as well, as I've gone through quite a few. Here's what happened to them all:

1ST	Wore a bit thin.
2ND	Exiled.
3RD	Poisoned.
4TH	Fell off a big telescope.
5TH	Poisoned again.
6TH	Fell off an exercise bike (I think).
7TH	Shot.

Ooh, I got a new body that day as well. Mine was better.

8TH	Drank dodgy potion.
THE WARRIOR	Wore a bit thin again.
9TH	Absorbed entire time vortex.
10TH	Exterminated.
10TH AGAIN	Poisoned again.
11TH	Got old, shouted at some Daleks, got young again, became me.

CYBERMEN V

Who would win in a battle between the Doctor's two biggest enemies? Choose a victor in each category below, then add up the points to see who is your overall winner!

HUMAN WEAPONRY IS NOT EFFECTIVE AGAINST CYBER TECHNOLOGY!

Missy's Cybermen have built-in guns, but others can kill with electricity from their hands!	WEAPONS
Cybermen can convert everyone on a planet – alive or dead! A single Cyberman could defeat a whole Earth city.	ARMIES
Cybermen share one giant hive mind, so they're all as smart as each other.	INTELLIGENCE
Superhuman speed. Rocket-powered boots allow them to blast up into the sky.	MOVEMENT
Steel armoured exoskeleton that can repair itself if it's damaged.	ARMOUR
Most weaknesses have been eliminated, but some Cybermen are allergic to gold.	WEAK SPOT
Cyber-Warships are scattered across the galaxy, full of many types of Cybermen.	FLEET
None.	EMOTIONS

CYBER FACTS

HOME PLANET: Earth
ORIGINAL SPECIES: Human
CREATOR: Missy
WHAT'S INSIDE? A real human brain! Ugh!

Missy created the most recent Cyber army, but there have been many others.

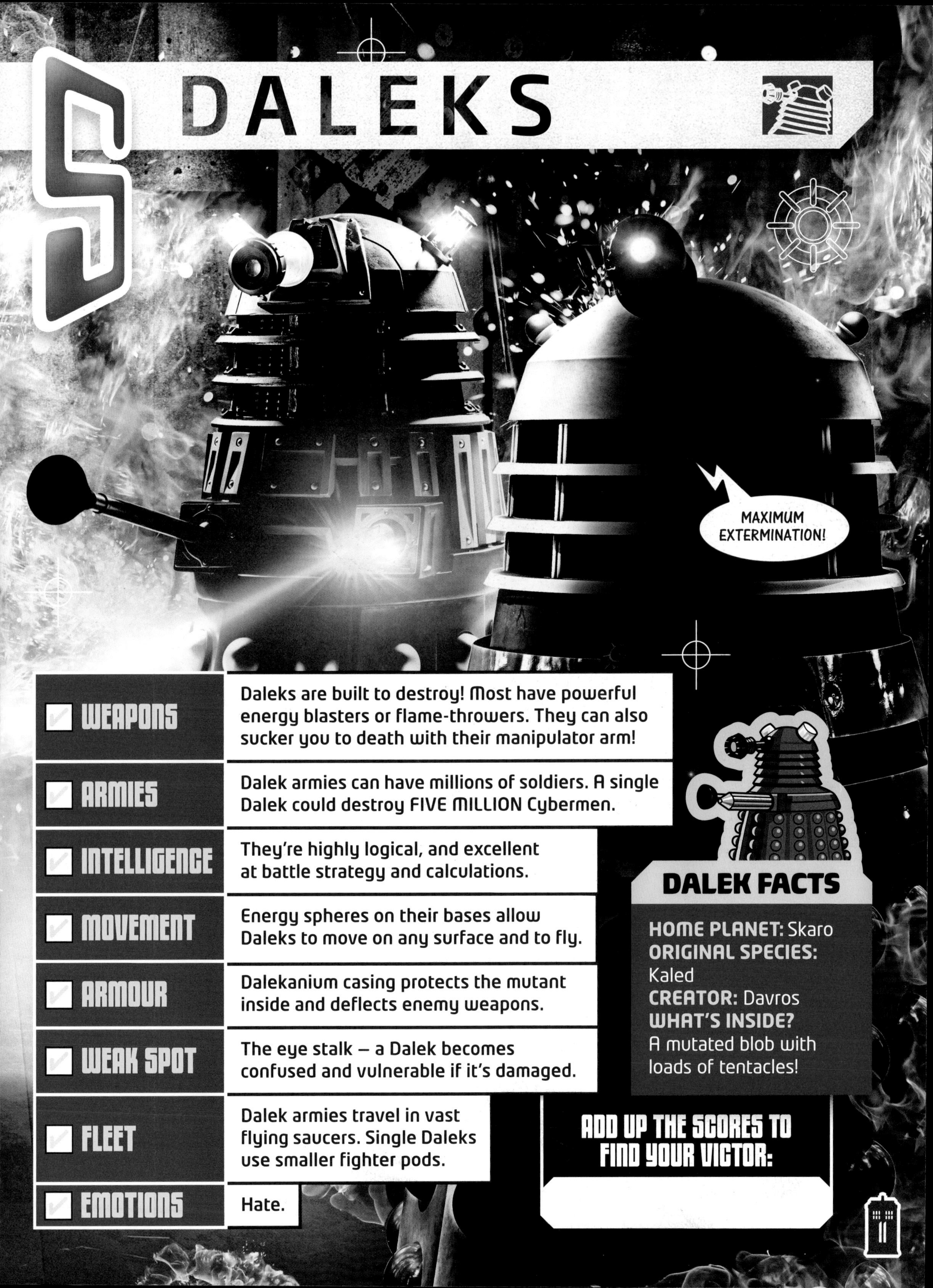

5 DALEKS

WEAPONS	Daleks are built to destroy! Most have powerful energy blasters or flame-throwers. They can also sucker you to death with their manipulator arm!
ARMIES	Dalek armies can have millions of soldiers. A single Dalek could destroy FIVE MILLION Cybermen.
INTELLIGENCE	They're highly logical, and excellent at battle strategy and calculations.
MOVEMENT	Energy spheres on their bases allow Daleks to move on any surface and to fly.
ARMOUR	Dalekanium casing protects the mutant inside and deflects enemy weapons.
WEAK SPOT	The eye stalk – a Dalek becomes confused and vulnerable if it's damaged.
FLEET	Dalek armies travel in vast flying saucers. Single Daleks use smaller fighter pods.
EMOTIONS	Hate.

DALEK FACTS

HOME PLANET: Skaro
ORIGINAL SPECIES: Kaled
CREATOR: Davros
WHAT'S INSIDE? A mutated blob with loads of tentacles!

ADD UP THE SCORES TO FIND YOUR VICTOR:

BREAK THE CLOISTER CODE

Use the Gallifreyan key to decode this secret message from the Matrix, and tell the Doctor who is trying to attack him!

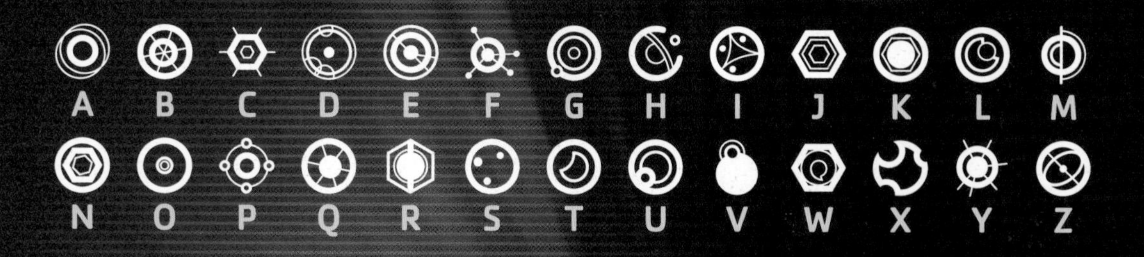

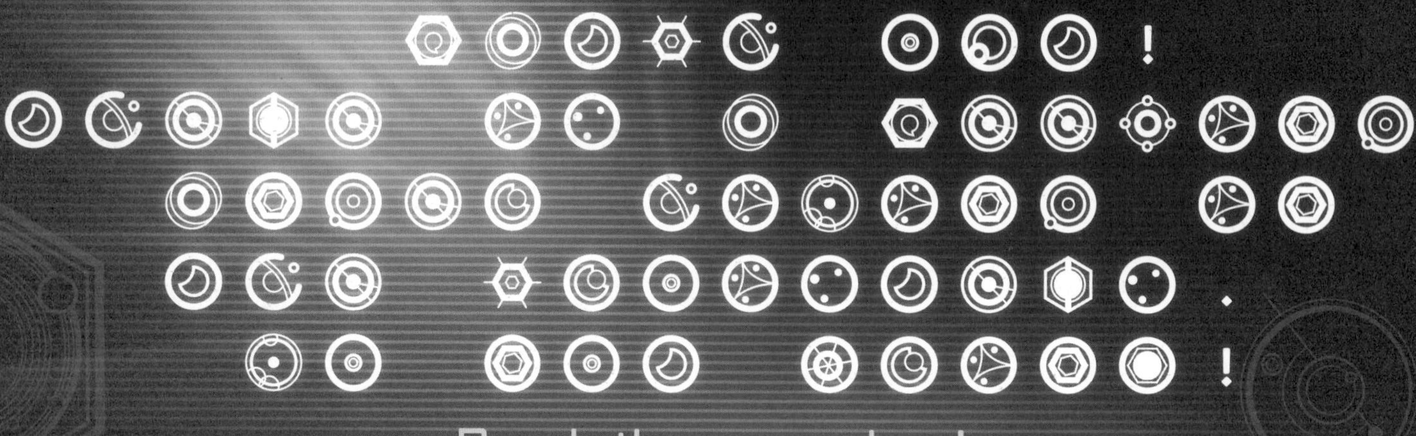

Decode the message here!

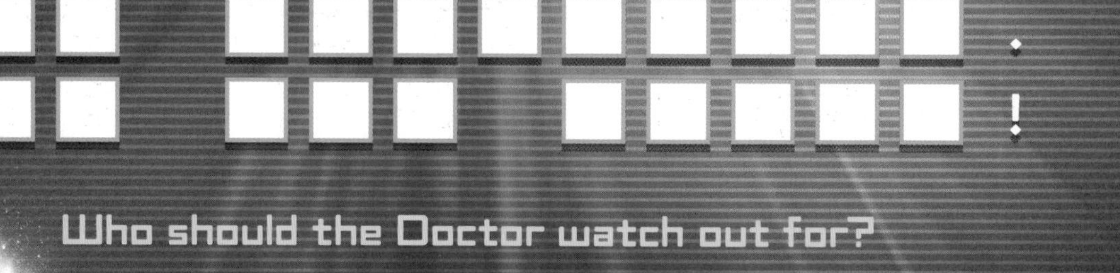

Who should the Doctor watch out for?

CYBER COLOURING IN

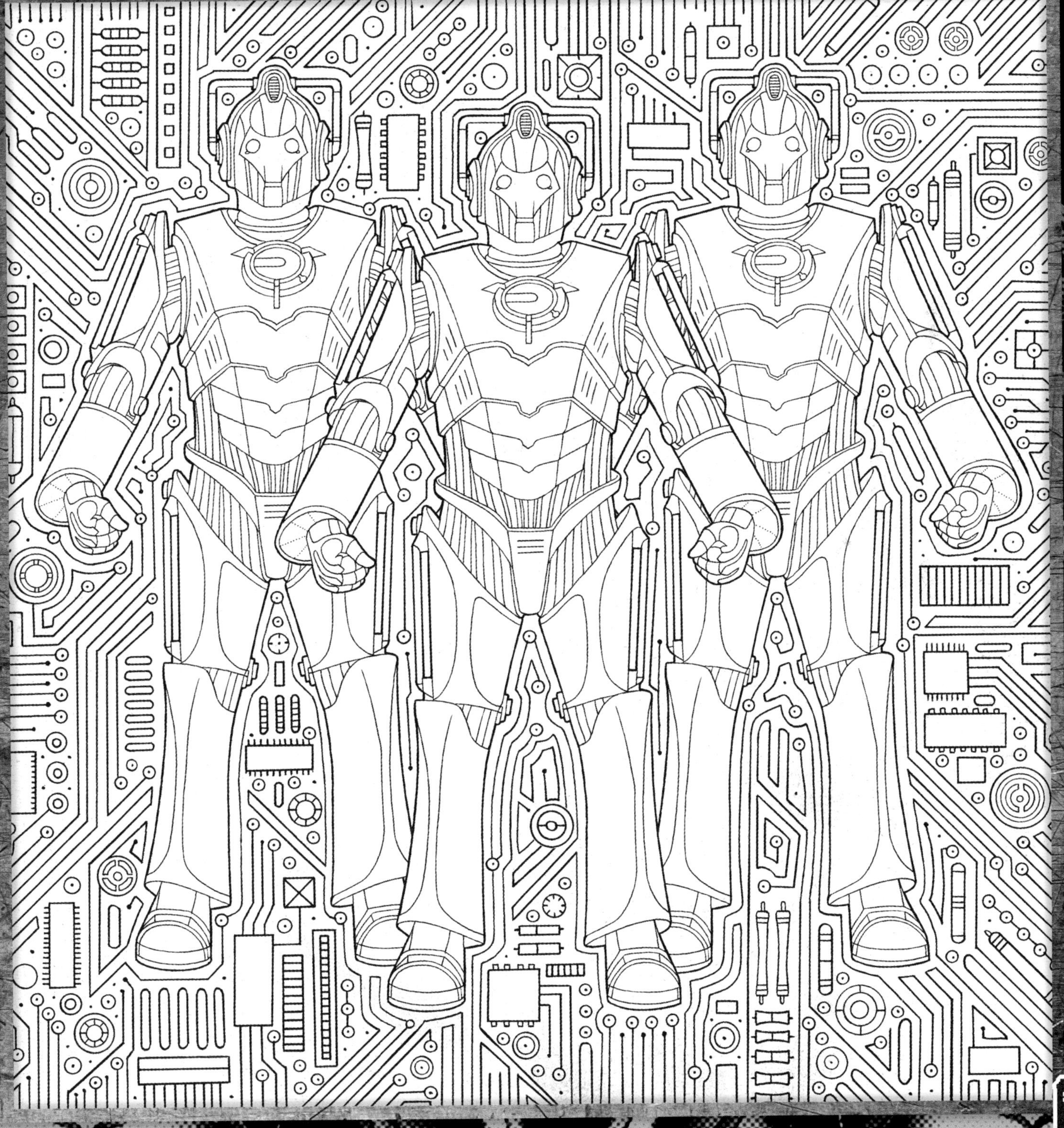

GALLIFREY

Planet of the Time Lords

What is it?

The Doctor's home planet – the Shining World of the Seven Systems.

Where is it?

Originally in the constellation of Kasterborous at ten-zero-eleven-zero-zero by zero-two from galactic zero centre.

What does it look like?

A giant, red planet, much bigger than Earth.

What happened to it?

The whole planet and everyone on it was thought to have been destroyed in the Time War, but the Doctor used stasis cubes to hide it away in a pocket universe.

Where is it now?

Billions of years in the future.

Around Gallifrey

THE CITADEL

A vast, glittering city under a mighty glass dome. Damaged in the Time War, but has since been restored, and is home to the President and the High Council.

ARCADIA

Gallifrey's second city, destroyed in a ferocious battle on the last day of the Time War. This dark day was captured in a painting, *Gallifrey Falls No More*.

THE DRY LANDS

The barn where the Doctor slept as a child is in this sandy, desert area of the planet near the Citadel.

Cloister Wraiths

When Time Lords die, their minds are uploaded into a giant, living computer called the Matrix. It's so powerful that it can predict the future!

It's guarded by Cloister Wraiths – projections of dead Time Lords, with the same robes and headdresses, but extra tall and very scary. They glide along the floor, so some Time Lords call them 'Sliders'.

The Wraiths are woken by the Cloister Bells, which ring when the Matrix forecasts danger! They haunt the Cloisters to put off anyone who wants to steal Time Lord secrets.

Daleks, Cybermen and Weeping Angels have all tried and failed to sneak past the Wraiths – any creatures they catch are filed away forever!

Time Lords

Gallifrey is ruled by the Time Lords – humanoids with two hearts and the ability to regenerate. But they're not all like the Doctor . . .

Rassilon was once a hero, but became ruthless and cruel during the Time War. The Doctor ordered him away from Gallifrey forever.

Missy and the Doctor grew up together on Gallifrey, but looking into the time vortex as a child made her go insane!

The General is Gallifrey's chief military commander. She's only been a man once in her eleven lives.

THE OSGOOD FILES

I'm Petronella Osgood, a scientist working with the Unified Intelligence Taskforce under Kate Stewart.

I'm also Petronella Osgood, a scientist working with the Unified Intelligence Taskforce under Kate Stewart. Don't look so confused.

UNIT was infiltrated by Zygon invaders – those chaps with the suckers on the next page. They can assume the form of other beings, and one of them became an Osgood, meaning there were two of me.

Eventually, twenty million Zygons settled on Earth as part of Operation Double. Humans and Zygons lived together in peace – for a while anyway. Then Missy killed one of us Osgoods. The one who was left never told anybody whether she was human or Zygon, to make sure the peace treaty was upheld.

The remaining Osgood was kidnapped by rogue Zygons and a rebellion started. The Zygons were tired of hiding, and things got pretty scary. But the Doctor sorted everything out, as usual.

The leader of the revolt, Bonnie, decided the best way to maintain the peace was to become an Osgood herself. So now there are two of us again! And no, we're still not going to tell you which is which.

Both of us Osgoods are BIG fans of the Doctor, so we want to know everything we can about him – and his enemies. We know you're a fan too, so we can trust you with our secret files!

THE ZYGONS

PROFILE:
Species: Zygon
Planet of origin: Zygor
Form: Shape-shifters

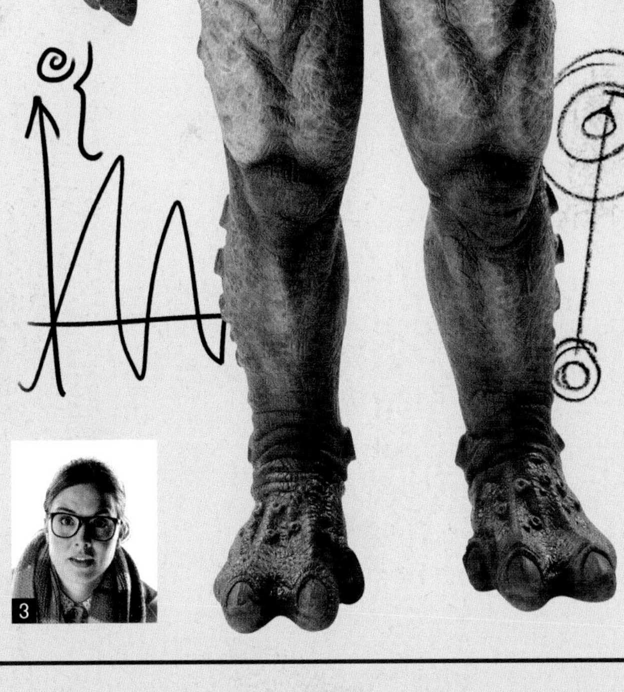

INTELLIGENCE REPORT:

When the Zygon home world was destroyed in the Time War, millions of Zygons came to Earth in search of a new home.

At first they wanted to take Earth by force – and they were well equipped to do so. Advanced body-print tech lets them take the form of anyone they scan – alive or dead!

They're pretty amazing physically, too. Venom sacs in their mouths, plus electrical charges in their hands that can stun or even melt someone away to a ball of skin, like a tumbleweed.

They're pretty intimidating – tall, with giant heads and bodies covered in suckers.

Physical strength, high intelligence, amazing technology – the Zygons have the lot!

CLASSIFIED INFORMATION:

Zygons once had to keep the humans whose shapes they take alive in special tanks.

CONNECTIONS:

1. BONNIE
2. OSGOOD
3. OSGOOD

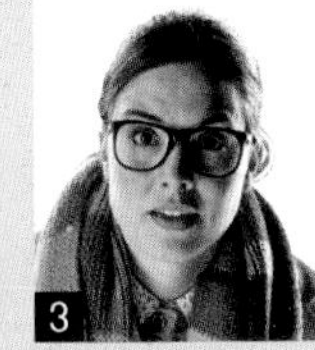

THE DOCTOR SAYS:

There were two Osgoods to police the ceasefire. One Zygon and one human to keep the secrets and keep the peace.

UNIT SIGHTING CONFIRMATION

Sign here if you have seen one or more Zygons:

The Adventures of Ashildr

AKA Me

WHO IS SHE?

A farmer's daughter living in a ninth-century Viking village.

WHAT HAPPENED TO HER?

Ashildr was killed helping to defeat the Mire, but the Doctor used their technology to repair her – meaning she could never die. Eventually she would forget her name, and all the other names she'd ever been called, becoming simply 'Me'.

HOW LONG DID SHE LIVE?

Until the very end of the universe! The Doctor met her again in the ruins of the Cloisters on Gallifrey, watching the stars as they died, one by one.

On the day the Great God Odin descended, our dear Ashildr, daughter of Einarr, went on her final journey to Valhalla. But this was not the end. The great magician, the Doctor, cast an enchantment and she returned to life. It was said by some that she would live forever . . .

Witnessed at the Battle of Agincourt, it was said that this fearsome soldier could fire six arrows in less than one minute . . .

I call myself Me. All the names I took died with whoever knew me. Me is who I am now. No one's mother, sister, daughter, or wife. My own companion. Singular, unattached. Alone.

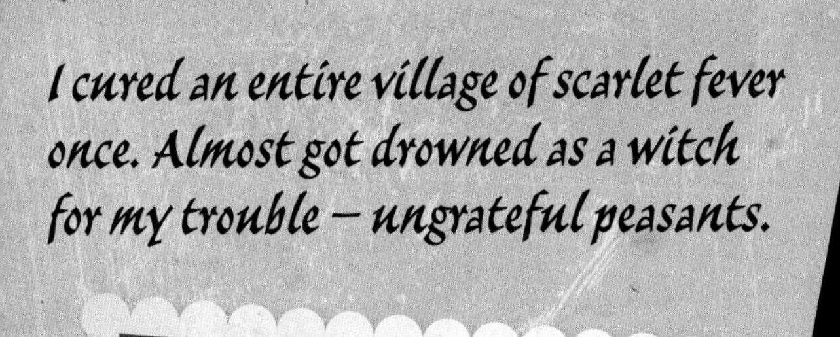
I cured an entire village of scarlet fever once. Almost got drowned as a witch for my trouble – ungrateful peasants.

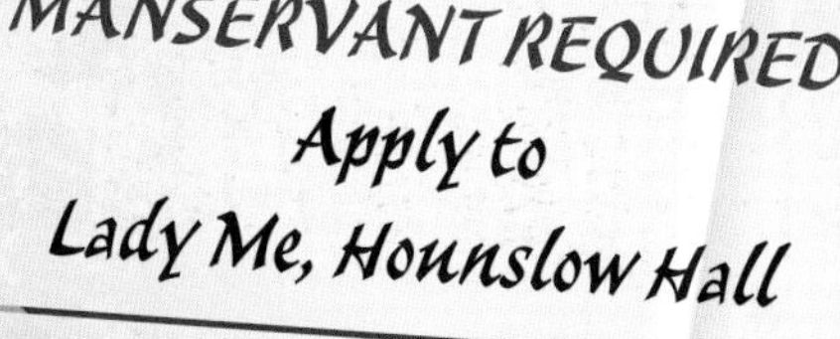
MANSERVANT REQUIRED
Apply to
Lady Me, Hounslow Hall

THE NIGHTMARE STRIKES AGAIN

- Robbery under cover of darkness
- Lucie Fanshawe takes to her bed in fright

Trap Street Times

MAYOR ME IN ALLIANCE WITH QUANTUM SHADE

- **Reports of Raven in flight**

Destination: GALLIFREY
Route: The long way round!

JOURNEY BACK TO EARTH
Throw a six to start. The first player to steer the TARDIS back to Earth is the winner.
A game for two or more payers. You'll need a dice and counters.
POLICE PUBLIC CALL BOX
1
2
3
4
5
6
7
MEET RIVER SONG ON DARILLIUM – MISS 2 TURNS.
9
10
11
12
13
ARGH! DALEKS! ROLL AGAIN.
15
YOU REACH THE WALL OF DIAMOND. START AGAIN.
17
18
19
20
21
22
23
24
25
26
THROW THE CORRECT NUMBER TO LAND ON EARTH!
68
67

MIRE ATTACK! MISS 2 TURNS.
28
HYDROFLAX CHASES YOU TO NO. 45!
30
31
32
CAUGHT BY COLONY SARFF! MISS A TURN.
34
35
36
37
THE TARDIS THROWS YOU FORWARD 6 PLACES.
POLICE BOX
39
40
41
42
CLOISTER WRAITHS CHASE YOU BACK TO NO. 21.
44
45
46
47
48
49
YOU MEET ASHILDR – THROW AGAIN!
51
FACE THE RAVEN! GAME OVER.
53
54
MISSY IS BLOCKING YOUR WAY! THROW A 2 TO MOVE.
56
57
58
59
60
61
WEEPING ANGELS SEND YOU BACK IN TIME TO NO. 5.
63
64
65
66

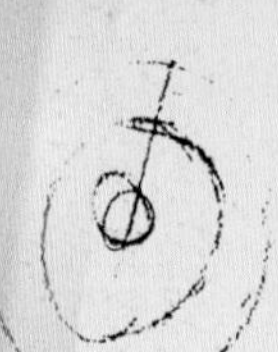

KING HYDROFLAX

PROFILE:

Full Name: His Infinite Majesty, King Hydroflax of the Final Cluster
Species: Human/Cyborg
Function: Tyrant

INTELLIGENCE REPORT:

Oh, this guy. He's a character. Brutish, humanoid face stuck on top of a giant, clanking metal body. Cyborg elements in the head, too.

That's the face of a killer if ever I saw one. The body bit's powered by a split quantum actualiser – a perpetually stabilised black hole. Clever stuff.

The head doesn't appear to be powered by much at all, though. And it's got a giant diamond lodged in it that could kill him at any second. River Song married him, but only to get the diamond.

Hydroflax ended up ordering the body to do anything necessary to survive. The body, being smarter, blasted him to smithereens and went solo.

CLASSIFIED INFORMATION:

CONNECTIONS:

1. RIVER SONG
2. NARDOLE
3. FLEMMING

1

2

3

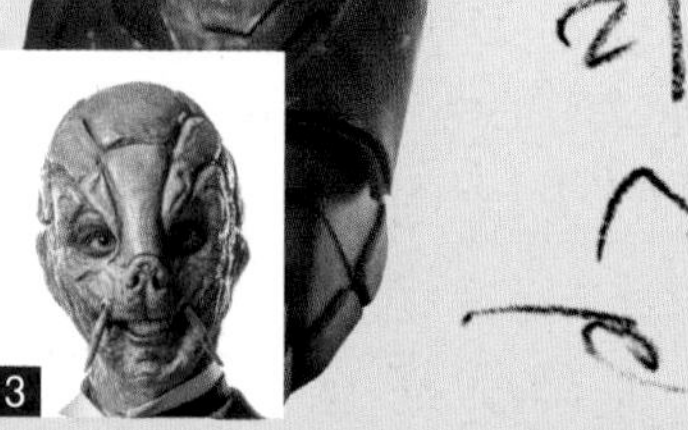

THE DOCTOR SAYS:

He's a mechanical man with a detachable head!

UNIT SIGHTING CONFIRMATION

Sign here if you have seen King Hydroflax:

ELEPHANT IN THE ROOM

AH.
THIS MAY NOT BE AS SIMPLE AS I'D HOPED.
IS THE DEADLY OBSTACLE COURSE STRICTLY NECESSARY?
SCHLERP!
THE KING GETS BORED. IT AMUSES HIM TO SEE US SLAVES SUFFERING.
REMIND ME TO HAVE A WORD WITH HIS MAJESTY BEFORE I LEAVE.
WAIT HERE. I'LL NIP ROUND THE COURSE AND WE'LL BE OFF IN NO TIME.

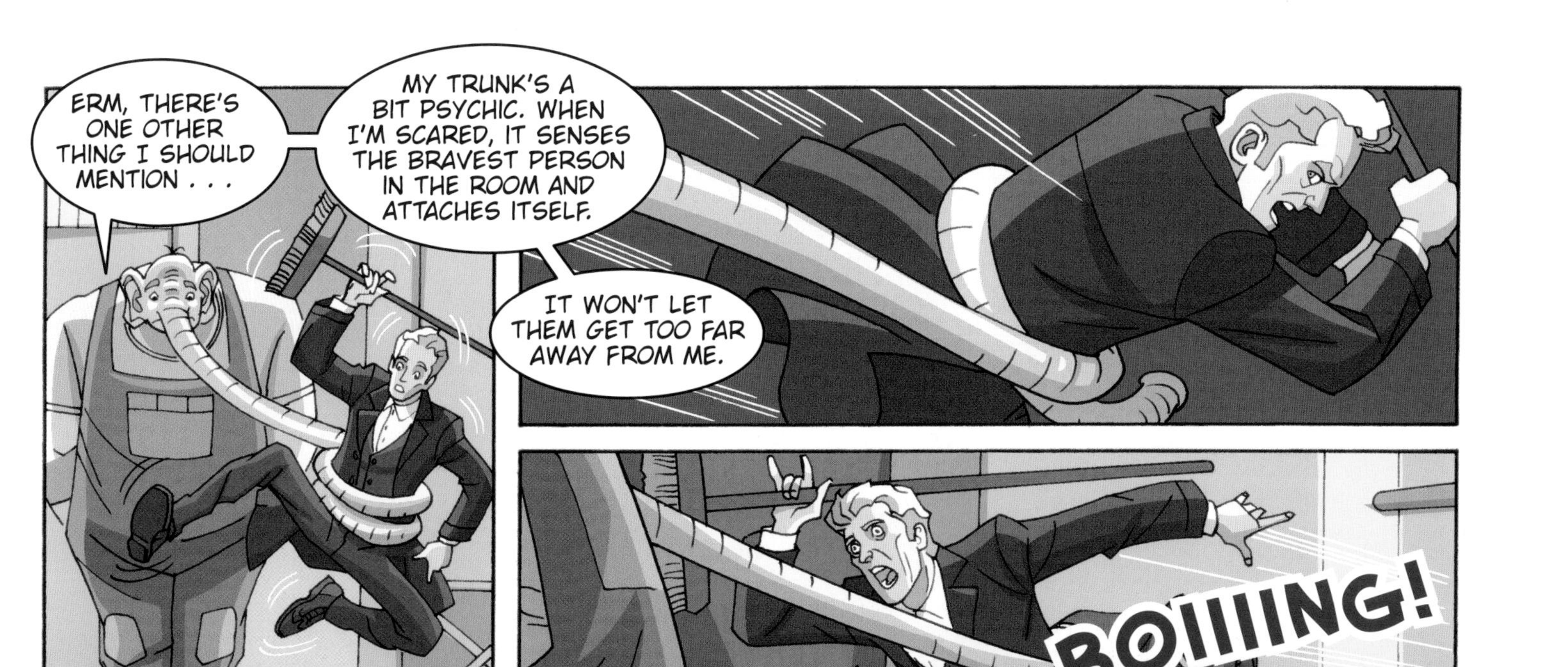
ERM, THERE'S ONE OTHER THING I SHOULD MENTION . . .
MY TRUNK'S A BIT PSYCHIC. WHEN I'M SCARED, IT SENSES THE BRAVEST PERSON IN THE ROOM AND ATTACHES ITSELF.
IT WON'T LET THEM GET TOO FAR AWAY FROM ME.
BOIIIING!
WAAAAAAH!

THEN YOU'LL HAVE TO COME WITH ME.
ME? B-BUT I'M TOO BIG! AND SO CLUMSY!
NONSENSE! YOU JUST NEED A BIT OF BALANCE!

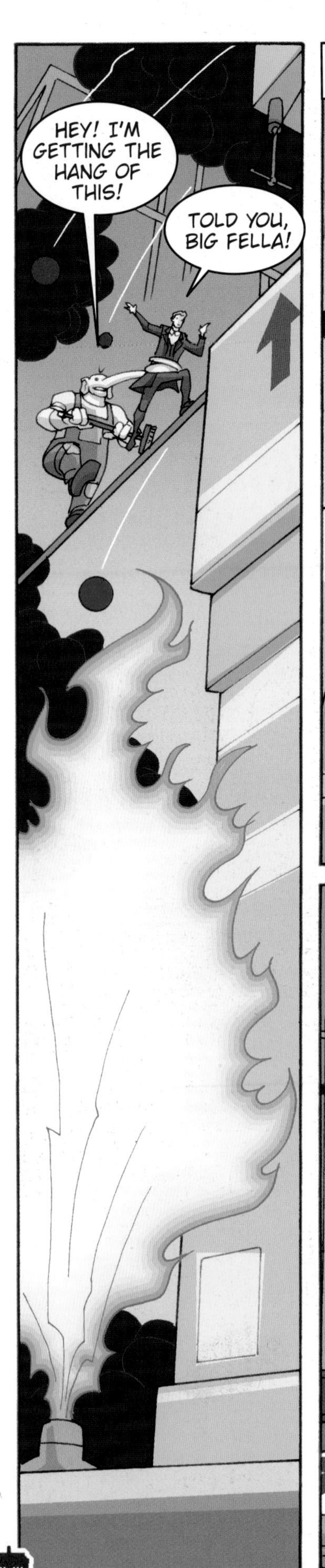
HEY! I'M GETTING THE HANG OF THIS!
TOLD YOU, BIG FELLA!

SOON, THEY REACH THE TOP . . .
READY?
I SUPPOSE SOOOOOOOOOOO!
THE MOMENTUM FROM THE SLIDE SHOULD GET US RIGHT UP TO THE TOP.
AS LONG AS WE HIT THE TRAMPOLINE AT THE RIGHT ANGLE . . .

AIM FOR THE BIG, RED X! THEN YOU'LL BOUNCE RIGHT UP!

BUT PROBOSCO MISSES!
WOOOOOAH!

DOCTOR! WE'RE GOING TO FALL!
NO, WE'RE NOT - AND I'LL TELL YOU WHY!

PROBOSCO IS PULLED BACK . . .
BOIIIING!
MY TRUNK!
YOU SAID IT WAS PSYCHIC. IT SENSED THE DANGER AND KEPT US TOGETHER!

WHAT NEXT?
ONCE I'M IN POSITION, YOU DROP.

HERE I GOOOOOOOOOOO!

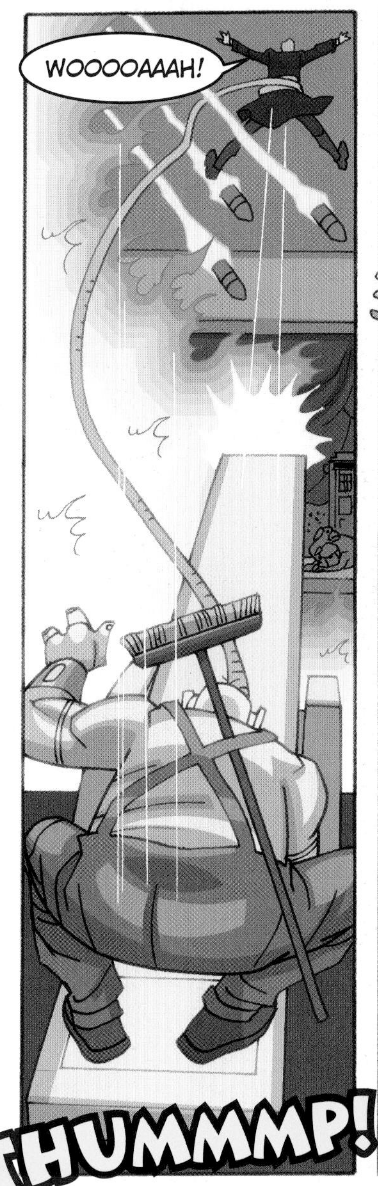
WOOOOAAAH!
THUMMMP!

BOIIIING!
POLICE PUBLIC CALL
BOX
WE MADE IT! AND LOOK! MY TRUNK!
MAYBE I'M NO LONGER THE BRAVEST PERSON IN THE ROOM. COME ON - LET'S GO!

SUDDENLY . . .
AH. I FORGOT ABOUT YOU.
DON'T WORRY, DOCTOR - I'VE GOT THIS COVERED!

FETCH, BOY!

YOU'RE OFF, THEN? SIGH. I'D BETTER GET BACK TO WORK.
THIS MESS WON'T CLEAN ITSELF UP.

NO, PROBOSCO. YOU'RE FREE NOW, AND I'M TAKING YOU HOME.

RIGHT AFTER I'VE DEALT WITH THE KING . . .
THE END

CALLING ALL AGENTS!

WE MUST RECOVER THE OSGOOD BOX!

Help Kate and the UNIT troopers get to the Osgood Box, avoiding Bonnie and the Zygons.

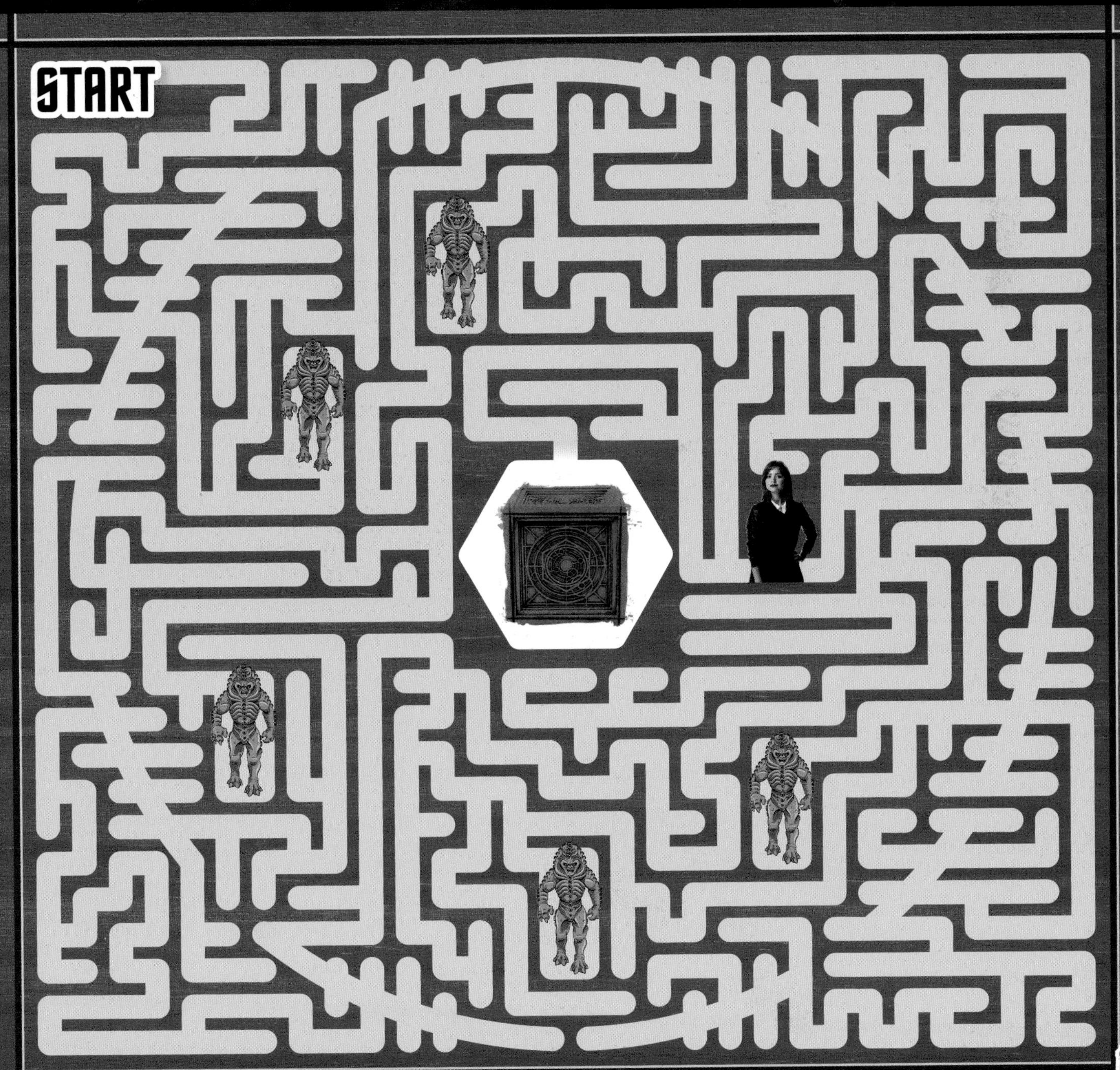

The Timey-Wimey Travels of RIVER SONG

MY LIFE WITH THE DOCTOR IS SO COMPLICATED EVEN I STRUGGLE TO KEEP TRACK!

7
I was taken to an orphanage on Earth. The Silence brainwashed me to kill the Doctor.

9
But I escaped and lived on the streets of New York. Life was tough – I got sick and regenerated. (Oh yes, forgot to mention – I'm part Time Lord!)

10
I was born in the 52nd century on an asteroid called Demon's Run. My mother, Amy Pond, had been kidnapped by the Silence and taken there. She named me Melody.

12
New face, new name – Mels! I went to find my parents, Amy and Rory, and we grew up together.

13
I was shot and had to regenerate, then gave up the rest of my lives to save the Doctor. But it was fine. I mean, LOOK at me – why would I WANT to change?

14
As I recovered, the Doctor left me my diary – I use it to keep track of all the times we've met.

15
The Silence found me again and sent me back in time, in an astronaut suit, to kill the Doctor. Well obviously I wasn't actually going to do THAT. But it was a fixed point, so all of time collapsed when I refused. Oopsie!

16
The only way to fix things was to marry the Doctor, which suited me just fine! He told me the version of him I'd shoot was actually a robot with a miniaturised version of him inside.

18
I still went to prison for the Doctor's 'murder'. But he would visit at night – we'd go off on wonderful adventures in the TARDIS, and I'd be back by morning.

My father asked me to join the battle at Demon's Run. I had to refuse – after all, I was already there, as a baby!

11

Then I got a special invitation from the Doctor – to his death! I had to pretend to Amy and Rory that I didn't know what was going on as my younger self, in the suit, seemed to kill the Doctor.

6

We finally defeated the Silence, and the Doctor and I kissed for the first time. Well, it was the first time for him anyway . . .

8

I went to Roman Britain in 102AD, posing as Cleopatra to deliver a message. I think I made a rather good Queen of the Nile!

4

I helped the Doctor fight the Pandorica Alliance, and got trapped in an exploding TARDIS for my trouble. Oh, he knows how to treat a girl, my old man!

5

The Doctor had a new face next time we met, so I didn't recognise him. By now, my diary was nearly full, so when we crashed on Darillium I feared my time was almost up. But the Doctor had neglected to tell me that one night on Darillium lasts for twenty-four years!

20

I saw my parents for the last time when they were cast back in time by the Weeping Angels. I promised my mother I'd be a good girl.

19

My poor parents still thought the Doctor had been killed by the astronaut, so I popped back and told them the truth.

17

I saw the Doctor and Amy again at the Crash of the Byzantium – though for my mother, this was the first time we'd met. The Doctor told me our last night together would be on the planet Darillium.

3

And lastly, our first meeting, in the Library. Sadly it was the last for me, as I died there. But even that wasn't as bad as looking into the Doctor's eyes and seeing that he didn't recognise me.

1

So if I'm dead, how can I be telling you this? Well, with the Doctor, death is never really the end. He uploaded my mind into a computer, where I lived on as an echo. But that can't last forever. I'll fade in the end – but please, don't tell me how or when . . .

2

Shhhh! Spoilers!

21

Starting at number 1, follow the yellow numbers to see the order in which the Doctor met River!

IT'S A TINY BIT COMPLICATED – USUALLY, PEOPLE NEED A FLOW CHART.

SECRETS OF THE DALEK LABORATORY

I, Davros, pledge that this is a whole and true study. It is to be used in the event of my death to ensure the survival and purity of the Dalek race.

BEHOLD! MY CREATIONS!

My people were on the brink of destruction, fighting a war we could not win. Drastic action was required. I accelerated their genetic mutation and placed them in armoured travel machines, with on-board battle computers for tactical brilliance.

I equipped them with weapons and tools. A basic firearm and a powerful cutting device. Fire. Excellent.

The Dalek cortex vault is one of my most elegant designs. It's an electronic brain designed specifically to keep hatred pure and burning, eliminating any tiny glimmer of kindness and compassion.

Antibodies swarm around the interior, protecting against damage and infiltration. Anything they find is reduced to dust, and the dust sustains the creature.

I also gave them a more powerful weapon than any physical one: the need to conquer and destroy, planted deep within every cell of their being!

My Daleks have a strong concept of home. They have rebuilt Skaro time and time again as a symbol of their strength and power.

The Daleks have a genetic defect, one I have been unable to eliminate – mercy for me, their father. I am connected to the life force of every Dalek, and they will do anything to protect my life.

All through time, the Doctor and I have been on the opposite sides of a war. Imagine the creature we might have created if we'd put our differences aside. A true hybrid! Two great warrior races, together creating a warrior greater than either. And now that I have stolen the regeneration energy of the Time Lords, who knows what might be possible?

The Daleks represent my lifetime's work. I believe, for the ultimate good of the universe, I was right to create them. Others disagree and say they are a force for evil, but this cannot be correct. They are life in its ultimate form. All other creatures are inferior, and must be destroyed. Exterminated. **EXTERMINATE!**

The Zooniverse

The Whoniverse is full of all sorts of incredible creatures . . . Find out about the animal-like friends and enemies the Doctor has come across on his travels!

LEANDRO

Species: Leonian

Leandro was from Delta Leonis, a star in Sigma Leoni. He told the Doctor his tribe had been overthrown and his wife killed, leaving him trapped on Earth with Ashildr. But he actually planned to open a portal to Earth to allow an army of Leonians to invade! When Ashildr realised this, she closed the portal. The other Leonians killed him, furious that he had failed.

MADAME VASTRA

Species: Homo Reptilia

The Doctor's friend Vastra was in hibernation with the other Silurians when tunnellers building the London Underground accidentally woke her up. She's a skilled warrior with lightning reflexes, and has a venomous tongue that she can extend like a whip. Like many other lizards, she's a carnivore, and has even been known to eat humans.

OTHER CREEPY CREATURES!

The Macra
Giant crabs that lived in the tunnels under New Earth.

The Zarbi
Massive ants from the planet Vortis.

JUDOON

Species: Judoon

These tall, thick-skinned creatures resemble rhinoceroses. They have small brains, best suited to logical, repetitive tasks. This means they are often employed as mercenaries or intergalactic police. Large lung capacity allows them to breathe even where oxygen levels are low.

SISTERS OF PLENITUDE

Species: Catkind

The Sisters were cat nuns who helped the sick on New Earth. They could cure any illness – but only because they were growing human clones and infecting them with all kinds of nasties to develop medicines! They were humanoid, but had cat fur and sharp, retractable claws.

CYBERSHADES

The Cybermen, trapped in Victorian London, stole brains from cats and dogs for these primitive Cyber-conversions. They scuttled on all fours like animals, and could obey basic commands, just like a well-trained pet! Don't even think about trying to outrun one – they're very speedy and can even climb up walls.

Tetraps

Bat creatures with eyes in the backs of their heads!

The Empress of the Racnoss

Giant spider hibernating at the centre of the Earth!

THE MIRE

PROFILE:
Full Name: Odin
Species: Mire
Function: Leader of the Mire

INTELLIGENCE REPORT:

Now, this lot are interesting. Advanced technology, most of it stolen from other races. And he's a Viking, isn't he? He definitely LOOKS like a Viking!

Osgood, you of all people should know a thing isn't always a thing just because it looks like a thing! That one's their leader, and he's just pretending to be Odin, the Viking god, so the real Vikings will do what he says. It's all holographic!

Makes sense. The other Mire look a bit like Vikings too, with the helmets and all that.

Those aren't just for decoration, though. They carry vials of liquid, freshly squeezed from their conquests. They scan them, pick the bravest and boldest, then nick all their hormones.

Oooh, nasty! So, testosterone, adrenaline, all the good stuff. And they drink it when they go into battle? Like a smoothie?

Exactly! Swords crackling with electricity, helmets full of hormones. All their other gear is in the helmets too. Plasma cannons, holo tech, medical kits. Disable the the helmet and you've got 'em!

CLASSIFIED INFORMATION:

Mire helmets can be programmed to repair humans.

CONNECTIONS:

1. MIRE WARRIORS
2. ASHILDR
3. VIKINGS

THE DOCTOR SAYS:

They're called the Mire. One of the deadliest warrior races in the galaxy.

UNIT SIGHTING CONFIRMATION

Sign here if you have seen Odin and the Mire:

WHO SAID WHAT?

HELP ME REMEMBER WHO SAID ALL THIS STUFF. I MEET A LOT OF PEOPLE, I CAN'T KEEP TRACK OF IT ALL!

1 'AT THE END OF EVERYTHING, ONE MUST EXPECT THE COMPANY OF IMMORTALS.'

OHILA ☐

ASHILDR ☐

DAVROS ☐

2 'YOU CAN'T FIGHT THEM, DOCTOR. THERE'S NO POINT. THEY'RE THE FUTURE. A NEW LIFE FORM. A BETTER LIFE FORM.'

DAVROS ☐

RASSILON ☐

RASMUSSEN ☐

3 'THE MAN WHO GAVE ME THIS WAS THE SORT OF MAN WHO KNEW EXACTLY HOW LONG A DIARY YOU WERE GOING TO NEED.'

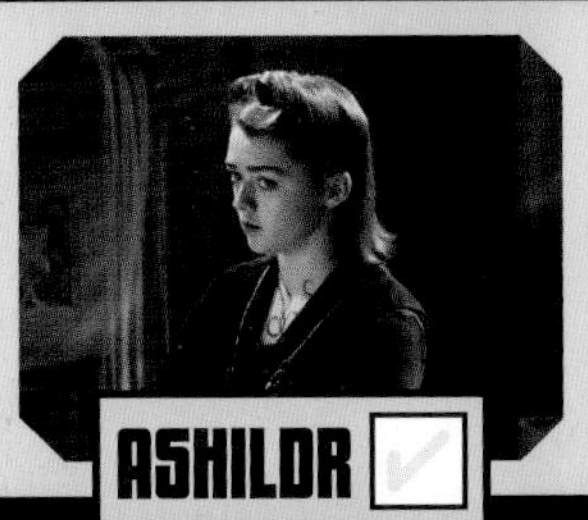

ASHILDR ☐

RIVER SONG ☐

CLARA ☐

4 'I DID WORSE THINGS THAN YOU COULD EVER IMAGINE, AND WHEN I CLOSE MY EYES . . . I HEAR MORE SCREAMS THAN ANYONE COULD EVER BE ABLE TO COUNT!'

THE DOCTOR ☐

DAVROS ☐

MISSY ☐

5 'MY FIRST PROPER ALIEN AND HE'S AN IDIOT.'

BENNETT ☐

PRENTIS ☐

O'DONNELL ☐

6 'OK, CUTTING TO THE CHASE: NOT DEAD, BACK, BIG SURPRISE, NEVER MIND.'

MISSY ☐

CLARA ☐

ASHILDR ☐

2

25 September 2016
Subject: New Head
To: **All Pupils** From: **Mr Myers**

Please assemble in the hall tomorrow morning at 8.55 a.m. to meet the new temporary head, Miss Magister. Latecomers will be severely punished.

1

18 September 2016
Subject: Saxon Heights
To: **Mum** From: **Ruby Baker**

Hi Mum! I can't believe it's been a week already! I thought I'd feel weird, coming to boarding school and being away from home, but it's been so amazing. I couldn't believe it when I saw Saxon Heights for the first time. It looked like an actual castle – so different from my old place! I've made loads of friends already, and even the teachers are cool. I really like the head, Mrs Goss. She's a bit old and batty, and her cardigan always seems to be covered in cat hair, but she's so funny. Lessons are fun too. We've got no pens and paper, it's all done on tablets! I'm using mine to email you. Anyway, gotta go – it's dinner time, then we're all going to watch YouTube videos. Bye for now!

Ruby

20 September 2016
Subject: Re: Saxon Heights
To: **Mum** From: **Ruby Baker**

Hey! Sorry I didn't get a chance to email yesterday. Loads has been happening! The big news is that poor old Mrs Goss is in hospital! She didn't turn up for assembly this morning so Mr Myers went to look for her and she was just sitting there, in her office, staring into space – like she'd been hypnotised or something. They've taken her to hospital to find out what's wrong.

Ruby

3

26 September 2016
Subject: Weirdness
To: **Mum** From: **Ruby Baker**

Today was strange. Like, REALLY strange. We all had to go to the hall to see the new head. She's not like any teacher I've ever seen before. She dresses weird, like she's Mary Poppins or something, in a big, frilly dress and funny hat with loads of berries on it. And she carries this little umbrella with her everywhere she goes. I think she must shop at that vintage place in town . . .

When she introduced herself, she did this weird jazz-hands thing, like she was waiting for a round of applause. It was mega-awks. We all said 'Good morning, Miss!' like we always did with Mrs Goss, but Miss Magister looked really angry.

'Don't call me Miss,' she said. 'It's "Good morning, Missy!"'
So. Weird.

Ruby

4

31 September 2016
Subject: Standards, or the lack thereof
To: **All Pupils** From: **Miss Magister**

Good morning, ladies! It has come to my attention that the standards of uniform and behaviour at this school are a disgrace.
A new uniform policy will be in place from today, comprising the following items:
- Plum skirt suit. Skirt cut to ankle length.
- Black ankle boots with sharp toe.
- White blouse with puffed shoulders and starched collar.
- Cameo brooch with school crest.
- Umbrella with long, wooden handle (metal umbrellas not acceptable).
- Black boater hat with lots of berries on it. Angle: rakish.
- Hair to be worn up at all times.

Big hugs,
Miss Magister

5

31 September 2016
Subject:
To: **Mum** From: **Ruby Baker**

She's totally lost the plot, Mum! She says we're not allowed to wear our own clothes any more, not even when we go to the shops. Can you believe it? I mean, where am I even going to get a plum skirt suit?

Other weird things are happening as well. All the prefects have been sent off to London on a school trip – something about inspecting the copies of Magna Carta . . . And there's something not quite right about the teachers. One minute they seem normal, but whenever SHE walks into the room, it's like they're somewhere else. Mum, I don't like it here any more – please can I come home?

Ruby

6

31 September 2016
Subject: Fwd:
To: **Dad** From: **Mum**

Haha, look at this, Dave! I'd love to see her in a plum skirt suit and fruity hat. I told you she'd find it tricky getting used to the rules at Saxon Heights . . . I'm sure she'll settle down by half term.

CONTINUED ON THE NEXT PAGE

Mail File Edit View Help

21 October 2016
Subject: Devices
To: **All Pupils** From: **Miss Magister**

You girls should count yourself lucky you can't see my face right now because it is NOT. HAPPY. All I see when I walk through this place is you lot, heads in your tablets, phones and whatnots, SnapBooking and FaceChatting. It's just soooooo tiresome. So, all mobile communications devices are banned. Yes, you heard me. BANNED. Please bring them all to my office no later than 8 p.m. tomorrow.

Toodle-oo!
Miss Magister

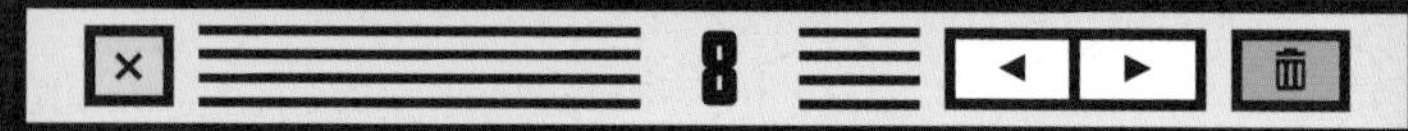

22 October 2016
Subject: Devices
To: **Mr Myers** From: **Miss Magister**

Device confiscation begins this evening. Would you be a dear and make sure they're all connected to the transmitter by midnight? Otherwise I'll be awfully cross, and you really won't like that. The big switch-on will be tomorrow, and then the fun times REALLY begin!

22 October 2016
Subject: I CAN'T EVEN
To: **Mum** From: **Ruby Baker**

OK, now Miss Magister has gone too far. She's taken everyone's tablets and phones! SO RANDOM. She says it's because we use them too much, but I think she's hiding something . . . Anyway, this has to be against my human rights! There's no way I'm giving my tablet up. I've hidden it under the bed, so if she wants it she can come and get it.

Ruby

10

22 October 2016
Subject: Unauthorised Wi-Fi receiver
To: **Mr Myers** From: **Miss Magister**

Oh Myersy-Wyersy, you've done it again, haven't you? You've let me down. My readings have just detected a rogue tablet, somewhere in the North Tower. Would you mind awfully popping up there to pick it up? Oh, and bring whichever brat is using it to my office. I've got a LOVELY surprise for her.

22 October 2016
Subject: ENCRYPTED MESSAGE
To: **Petronella Osgood**
From: **Petronella Osgood**

It's her! We've detected a massive increase in transmitter activity, localised at Saxon Heights boarding school, near Devil's End. She's either trying to summon up a Dæmon or she's got a lot of data that won't roll over to use up before the end of the month. I know which I think it is.

Recommend full recovery mission – contact Kate Stewart for authorisation!

12

23 October 2016
Subject: DRAMA
To: **Mum** From: **Ruby Baker**

OMG! Mum, you won't believe what's happened now.

I was marched out of lessons yesterday afternoon by Mr Myers and taken to the head's office. Miss Magister was mad. Really mad! Someone must have told her I hadn't handed in my tablet. She got all up in my face, snarling at me.

'I am the headmaster, and you will obey me,' she said.

'I thought you were the headMISTRESS,' I replied, which just seemed to make her even more angry. I told her she had no right to take everyone's phones, and she just laughed and called me a 'stupid, stupid child'.

The phones and tablets were all there, built up into a tower and all switched on. Then Miss Magister took out her own phone. At least I think it was a phone – it didn't have a screen, just two circles that were red and glowing.

'Ruby, Ruby, Ruby,' she said. 'What AM I going to do with you?'

I told her she could do what she liked – I didn't want to stay at her stupid school anyway. She laughed again, took a lipstick out of her pocket and started putting it on.

'Well, my dear, that is exactly what I wanted to hear. I think you're going to have to be excluded from Saxon Heights. Permanently excluded.' She lifted up her phone thing and held it up between us. Weird time to take a selfie, I thought.

She was just about to press the button when the office window smashed, and a soldier came swinging in on a rope!

23 October 2016
Subject: ENCRYPTED MESSAGE
To: **Kate Stewart** From: **Petronella Osgood**

Target has evaded capture again. No positive ID. Could have been her, but we can't say for certain.

24 October 2016
Subject: Revenge
To: **Ruby Baker** From: **Miss Magister**

OK, you got me this time. Well done you. It's not every fourteen-year-old girl who can get one over on me. But if you ever see me again, make sure you cross the road before I see you. And if we do come face to face? Well, just make sure you say something nice . . . 😍

A Day in the Life . . .

If you travel with the Doctor, you're in for danger and adventure all day long!

09:00AM

WAKE UP . . . AND STAY ALERT!

First things first – check for anything unusual in the sky. If you see planets, spaceships, or planes that don't seem to be moving, it's going to be a busy day!

11:30AM

WALK ACROSS CONTINENTS TO SAVE THE DOCTOR

When the Master conquered the Earth and held the Doctor prisoner for a whole year, Martha Jones refused to give up hope. She travelled all over the Earth, telling stories of the his bravery so nobody would forget him.

01:00PM

LUNCHTIME SHIFT AT THE DINER

Travel with the Doctor for long enough and something will probably happen to tear the two of you apart. He might even forget what you look like. So if he turns up at your TARDIS when it's disguised as a diner and tries to play you a sad song on his guitar, play dumb.

04:00PM

BIOLOGICAL METACRISIS, FOLLOWED BY A NAP

The Tenth Doctor kept a spare hand in a jar and it grew into an extra Doctor. Donna got caught up in it all and a human – Time Lord meta-crisis happened. The bonus Doctor was part Donna, and she became part Doctor. Her brain couldn't take it, though, and the Doctor had to take away all of Donna's memories of him.

07:00PM

DINNER . . . ON A DIFFERENT PLANET

After a hard day's adventuring, it's time to eat. Demand the best table in the restaurant overlooking the Singing Towers of Darillium, and make sure your waiter is a giant red robot.

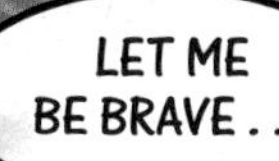

10:00PM

FACE THE RAVEN

Clara thought she was being clever when she took on Rigsy's chronolock to save his life. But when it couldn't be removed, the deadly Raven came looking for her instead. The Doctor rescued her, but she's stuck on her last heartbeat and must return to face the Raven again, one day.

12:00AM

BE PATIENT, LIKE THE GIRL WHO WAITED

Little Amelia Pond was terrified of a crack in her bedroom wall, so the Doctor promised to rescue her, right after he'd sorted out a problem with the TARDIS engines. She packed her bag and waited for him, but he didn't turn up a while – twelve years, to be exact!

02:00AM

SLEEP!

Finally! Watch out for Dream Crabs, though . . .

THE FISHER KING

PROFILE:
Full Name: The Fisher King
Species: Unknown
Function: Warlord

INTELLIGENCE REPORT:

Oh, he looks a bit like Uncle Charlie!

He does NOT! Uncle Charlie's not eight foot tall for a start! So how did he end up on Earth? Not another one who enslaved Tivoli?

'Fraid so. The people there just love being enslaved. It says in the file that the King ruled there for ten years until the planet was liberated by the Arcateenians. They thought he was dead so he was shipped to a 'barren, savage outpost'.

And that would be Earth, right? I wish people would stop doing that. Not dead though, I assume?

Nope. He killed people and turned them into transmitter ghosts who would lure his people to Earth to collect him. In the future, the Doctor saw a ghost version of himself so he nipped back in time to cause a massive flood. The Fisher King came from an arid and barren world, so water really wasn't his thing and that was the end of him.

CLASSIFIED INFORMATION:

The Fisher King's arm has a built-in blaster.

CONNECTIONS:

1. GHOST DOCTOR
2. PRENTIS
3. O'DONNELL

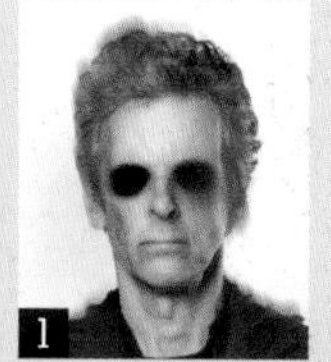
1

2

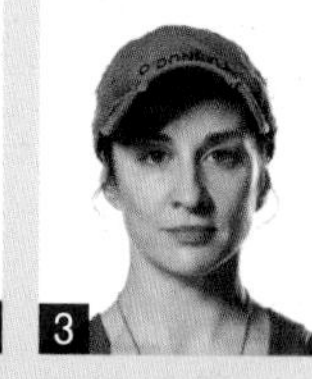
3

THE DOCTOR SAYS:

The Fisher King had been dead for one hundred and fifty years before we even got here!

UNIT SIGHTING CONFIRMATION

Sign here if you have seen the Fisher King:

THE PROMISE

OK. NOW I SEE WHY THEY CALL THIS PLACE THE FORBIDDEN ZONE.

OI! TINPOTS!

DOCTOR! THIS WAY, QUICK!
LAMBERT! JUST IN TIME!

SOON . . .
WE CAN'T LEAVE, DOCTOR. THIS WORLD IS RUINED, BUT OUR FAMILY IS HERE. IT'S STILL HOME.
I UNDERSTAND. BUT THERE IS SOMETHING I CAN DO.

IF YOU'RE EVER IN DANGER, KIRON, JUST THINK OF ME.
THIS WILL LET ME KNOW, AND I'LL COME BACK.

PROMISE?
I PROMISE!

MANY YEARS LATER . . .
WE SHOULDN'T BE OUT IN THE OPEN. IT'S DANGEROUS.
IT'S FINE, GLADVIS. WE'LL BE SAFE.

A HOWLER! KIRON!
DOCTOR!

AGAIN?! THAT BOY LOVES TROUBLE!

VWORP! VWORP!
HELP! HEEEEEEELP!
HA! DON'T WORRY, GLADVIS. I'M PROTECTED!

DOCTOR! I KNEW YOU'D COME. YOU ALWAYS DO!
A PROMISE IS A PROMISE, YOUNG MAN.
BUT I'VE WARNED YOU - DANGER WILL FIND YOU EASILY ENOUGH. DON'T GO LOOKING FOR IT.

WHO WAS THAT MAN?
MY FATHER SAVED HIS LIFE, SO HE PROMISED TO PROTECT MINE.

MANY MORE YEARS LATER . . .

IS IT TIME, GLADVIS?
YES. SUMMON HIM.

KIRON! WHAT'LL IT BE THIS TIME?
EXPLODING SCIENCE LAB?
FACING DOWN AN ENEMY KILLTANK?
WRESTLING AN OCTOBOT, SINGLE-HANDED?

WELL, THIS ISN'T WHAT I WAS EXPECTING.
YOU WILL ACCOMPANY ME TO PRESIDENT KIRON'S CHAMBERS.
POLICE BOX

OH, PRESIDENT KIRON NOW, IS IT? THE BOY DONE GOOD!

HAIL KIRON THE PROTECTED
SUDDENLY I'M NOT FEELING QUITE AS GOOD ABOUT ALL THIS . . .

AH, DOCTOR! I THOUGHT YOU'D NEVER GET HERE.
AND WHY AM I HERE, EXACTLY? YOU DON'T LOOK LIKE YOU'RE IN DANGER.

DOCTOR, I'M ALWAYS IN DANGER.
I'VE BROUGHT ORDER TO THE CHAOS OF THIS WORLD. BUT NOT EVERYONE LIKES MY . . . METHODS.
OH, REALLY? AND WHAT SORT OF METHODS ARE THEY?

EVERY TIME YOU PROTECTED KIRON, I FILMED IT. THE CLIPS SOON WENT VIRAL.
PEOPLE SAW THAT I WAS INVINCIBLE. MY POWER GREW. BUT THAT WASN'T ENOUGH.

SO I STUDIED THIS DEVICE. YOU INSTALLED A LOW-LEVEL TELEPATHIC LINK.
IT WAS EASY TO AMPLIFY IT - WATCH.

MOST OF THE TIME, THEY THINK THEY'RE FREE. IDIOTS!
BUT I CONTROL THEM.

THEY BUILT THE DOME, RESTORED THE CITY, ENSLAVED OUR ENEMIES - ALL AT MY COMMAND!

AND YOU THINK THIS IS GOOD, DO YOU?
YOU WERE PROTECTED. YOU HAD A CHANCE TO LIVE A GOOD LIFE, MAKE SOMETHING OF YOURSELF.

AND ***THIS*** IS WHAT YOU DID WITH THAT CHANCE?

WHY NOT? I'LL DO WHAT I LIKE. I'M PROTECTED. YOU PROMISED.
WELL, HERE'S A NEW PROMISE: I'LL STOP YOU!

I DON'T THINK SO, DOCTOR. I HAVE THIS ENTIRE PLANET AS MY ARMY. WHAT DO YOU HAVE?

I DON'T NEED AN ARMY - I CAN END YOU WITH JUST ONE WORD.
AND DO YOU KNOW WHAT IT IS?
NO!

NO! YOU NO LONGER HAVE MY PROTECTION.

THE SPELL IS BROKEN . . .
FWWWWWWWWWMPH!

GLADVIS, STOP THE BROADCAST!
KIRON! WHAT HAVE WE DONE?

DOCTOR! I'M SORRY! I'M SO SORRY!
WHAT DO I DO NOW? PLEASE!

DOCTOR! I NEED TO SET THINGS RIGHT. I . . . I NEED YOUR HELP!

THEN WE SHALL SET IT RIGHT. TOGETHER!
THE END.

THE VEIL

PROFILE:
Full Name: Unknown
Species: Unknown
Function: Unknown

INTELLIGENCE REPORT:

That's a LOT of unknowns.

The Time Lords are involved. Always very mysterious. When the Doctor was a boy, there was an old lady who died. They covered her in veils, but it was a hot day, and eventually the flies came. That's why the Veil makes that buzzing noise – the Doctor's had bad dreams about it ever since.

Oh, that's sad. So when he was trapped in the clockwork castle, his own dreams were used against him. But why?

So he would confess his deepest secrets. Every time he gave something away, the Veil would freeze, the castle would switch around, and he'd be one step closer to Room Twelve – the way out.

But did the Veil get him in the end?

Yes, every time. The Doctor died, over and over. But the castle wasn't a castle – he was actually inside his own confession dial, and could have left at any time if he'd 'fessed up to the Veil.

CLASSIFIED INFORMATION:

The azbantium wall in Room Twelve is four hundred times harder than diamond.

CONNECTIONS:

1. THE DOCTOR
2. CONFESSION DIAL
3. CLOCKWORK CASTLE

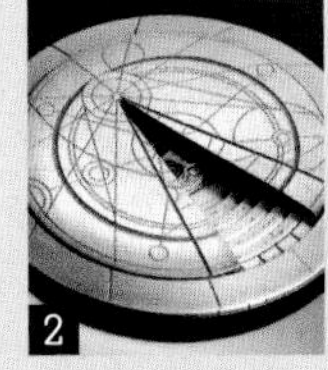

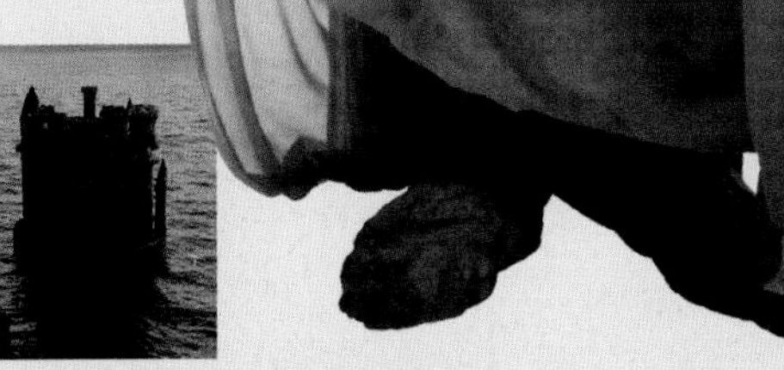

THE DOCTOR SAYS:

It's following me. Wherever I go, it's tracking me. Slowly and scarily lurching. Gives me the creeps . . .

UNIT SIGHTING CONFIRMATION

Sign here if you have seen the Veil:

The Next Adventure

The Doctor is visiting Coal Hill School! What happens next? This time, it's up to YOU to invent the Doctor's next adventure . . .

SO, YOU THINK YOU CAN TELL ME WHAT TO DO, EH?

Write the title of your adventure and your name here!

Written by:

The Doctor is here with a new friend, who is called:

And they look like this:

They are very:

- Brave
- Strong
- Clever
- Practical
- Funny
- Daring
- Kind
- Grumpy
- Tough
- Reliable
- Fearless
- Reckless
- Agile
- Argumentative
- Courageous
- Wise
- Crazy
- Truthful
- Quiet
- Patient
- Optimistic
- Pessimistic
- Angry

This is how the story starts:

It's a quiet morning at Coal Hill School . . .

Then something REALLY EXCITING happens. There's . . .

- An explosion
- A fire
- A chase
- An alien attack

Something else (write it here):

Then a TERRIFYING monster appears! The monster is called:

DRAW IT HERE!

It has . . .

- Heads
- Eyes
- Noses
- Arms
- Legs
- Tentacles
- Wings

The monster is made of . . .

- Flesh
- Stone
- Metal
- Something else (write it here):

Three need-to-know facts about this monster:

1
2
3

There's a SHOCKING twist, and the Doctor ends up:

- In the past
- In the future
- On an alien planet
- On a spaceship

Then everything changes when SUDDENLY . . .

Just when you least expect it, the Doctor invents a gadget which has the power to . . .

Eventually, the monster is defeated by . . .

And once again, the Doctor is ready to head off on another adventure!

RUN!

The Doctor's Greatest Escapes

ESCAPE SCORE

Score each of these amazing getaways out of five!

1. EASY – no effort whatsoever.
2. AVERAGE – slightly out of breath.
3. TRICKY – serious brain-power needed!
4. SUPER-SCARY – OK, this is getting impressive.
5. IMPOSSIBLE – HOW did he get out of that?

ANY QUESTIONS?

TAKING THE PLUNGE!

Episode:
The Zygon Inversion

Zygon Bonnie thought she'd got rid of the Doctor and Osgood when she blew up the plane they were on – but she didn't know he had a handy Union Jack parachute.

ESCAPE SCORE: 

FREEZER FEAR!

Episode:
Sleep No More

The Doctor, Clara and Nagata were trapped in a freezer with the Sandmen, with no way out! They only got away when the Doctor realised the creatures couldn't see a thing.

ESCAPE SCORE: 

I THINK THEY'RE BLIND . . .

STARSHIP SCRAMBLE!

Episode:
The Husbands of River Song

The Doctor and River were being held prisoner on board a spaceship about to be hit by a meteor strike. Luckily, they knew just the right place to stand so they could drop to freedom when the floor underneath them gave way. Sneaky!

ESCAPE SCORE: 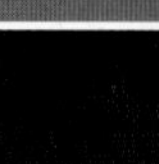

ULTIMATE TRAP!

Episode:
Heaven Sent

The Doctor, trapped in his own confession dial, lived through the same events over and over again, only to come up against a wall of solid diamond each time. All he could do was go round again and again for four and a half billion years until he chipped it all away!

ESCAPE SCORE:

ESCAPE FROM THE CLOISTERS!

Episode:
Hell Bent

Only one person ever escaped the Cloister Wraiths on Gallifrey – the Doctor! He got away when he was a student by going through a secret passage, then stealing a TARDIS. History repeated itself when the Time Lords cornered him in the Cloisters, and Clara distracted them while he nicked another TARDIS!

ESCAPE SCORE: 

TIME AND RELATIVE DIMENSION IN SEARCH

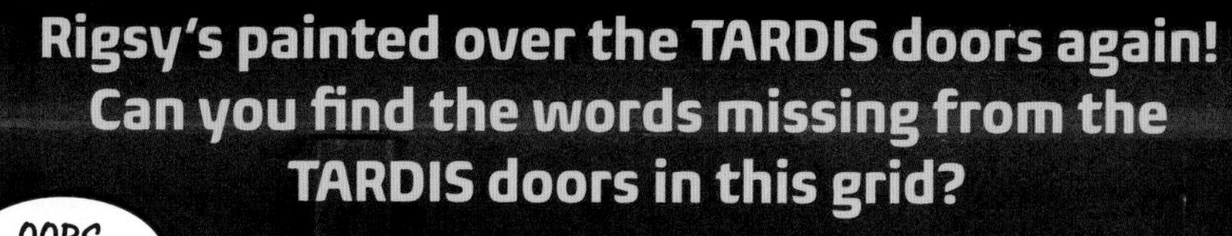

Rigsy's painted over the TARDIS doors again! Can you find the words missing from the TARDIS doors in this grid?

POLICE
TELEPHONE
FREE
FOR
USE
PUBLIC
ADVICE
ASSISTANCE
OBTAINABLE
IMMEDIATELY
OFFICERS
CARS
RESPOND
ALL
CALLS
PULL
OPEN

Cross out these words when you find them.

R U H X Q C E B C T W W N S K C U T C A L L S
H O O B T A I N A B L E K R J X E F E I A G X
U B F K P K E S A H W L L A H N G C C H V K K
L Q B E Z F N C X D R L K S O H N C X D P Q Y
M Y L H F J N X A A V B I H K A N N U U Z P Q
H V V L X E S U R R S I P T T I P O B F I Y Q
O Y K D U K S R R C S E C S F M P L G X W X I
H H I D Z P P E H P L L I E A Y I J U S K T Q
W O L F O D Q S T E P S K C L C V L R F R A Q
T P I D F O Y P T R S T I M M E D I A T E L Y
O K T E F N H O Y A B T B B E S C K J E E D Q
P G D C I E R N T L O X J N L W G I M X A F R
E Y O M C E Q D M P F Z M P J F E Y L L I B M
N H B L E R T O B J P N H E U R V J E O N H E
C Q Q N R F S H V O D J N L X K K K X P P M X
X D E K S E U U Z A Q Q G H Z W Y U J D F V L

THE SANDMEN

INTELLIGENCE REPORT:

Carnivorous life forms made from human sleep dust? Why would anyone invent those?

They were an accident, sort of. A scientist called Rasmussen invented Morpheus pods, which used an electronic signal to give people a whole month of sleep in just five minutes.

And let me guess – there were nasty side-effects and people started to die?

You're so good at this! Yes, the sleep dust started converting people into Sandmen – even Rasmussen himself, although he kept his human form. His plan was to film everything that was happening, and use that as a disguise to get everyone to watch the Morpheus signal.

So everyone who watched it would become a Sandman?

Exactly. So whatever you do, don't look!

PROFILE:

Biology: Human sleep dust
Aliases: Dust Men
Function: To spread the Morpheus infection through the galaxy

CLASSIFIED INFORMATION:

Warning! Before he died, Rasmussen transmitted a hidden Sandman signal!

CONNECTIONS:

1. RASMUSSEN
2. 474
3. NAGATA

THE DOCTOR SAYS:

We have to get to Triton. Destroy all the Morpheus machines. End this.

UNIT SIGHTING CONFIRMATION

Sign here if you have seen the Sandmen:

I SUPPOSE YOU THINK THAT'S IT, DO YOU? WELL, I'M HERE TO CHECK HOW CAREFULLY YOU HAVE BEEN READING THIS BOOK.

All the answers have appeared somewhere in these pages . . . But no turning back – that's cheating!

MONSTERS

1 What destroyed the Fisher King?

A] Water

B] Fire

C] Ice

2 What was the power source of King Hydroflax's robot body?

A] A split quantum actualiser

B] Clockwork

C] Black light

3 What's unusual about a Zygon's mouth?

A] It's got two tongues

B] It has green lips

C] It's venomous

FRIENDS

1 What was my granddaughter's name?

A] Susan

B] Tegan

C] Rose

2 What species is Madame Vastra?

A] Homo Superior

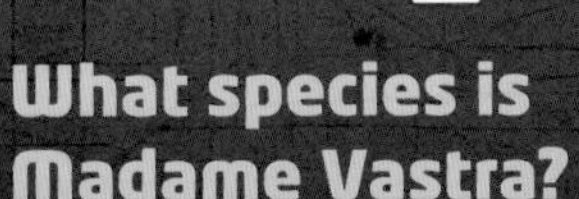

B] Homo Reptilia

C] Homo Sapiens

3 Where did I first meet River Song in my own timeline?

A] The Crash of the Byzantium

B] Darillium

C] The Library

TRUTH OR CONSEQUENCES

1. Clara Oswald was there when I first stole a TARDIS.

TRUE  FALSE

2. King Hydroflax had a diamond lodged in his head.

TRUE  FALSE 

3. Cybershades are dogs and cats converted by Cybermen.

TRUE  FALSE 

4. The Daleks are from Gallifrey.

TRUE  FALSE 

5. I saved Ashildr using Mire technology.

TRUE  FALSE 

ME

1. How many times did my tenth body regenerate?

A] Once

B] Twice

C] Three times

2. There was a wall in my confession dial, which I had to break down - what was it made of?

A] Concrete

B] Dalekanium

C] Azbantium

3. Who stole some of my regeneration energy to extend their own life?

A] Davros

B] Missy

C] Clara

PLANETS

1. What happened to Gallifrey, my home planet?

A] It was destroyed

B] I hid it in a pocket universe

C] It was sucked into a black hole

2. Where were the Sisters of Plenitude from?

A] Earth

B] Old Earth

C] New Earth

3. Who rebuilt Skaro?

A] The Daleks

B] Davros

C] Missy

FRIEND FROM THE FUTURE

Only two of these pictures of Bill and the Doctor are absolutely identical. Can you spot which ones they are?

WHAT'S A DALEK?!

A B C D E F G H

FIND THE SONIC SUNGLASSES

The sonic sunglasses are hidden on p. 7, p. 12, p. 16, p. 19, p. 29, p. 32, p. 41, p. 42, p. 55 and p. 60.

P. 12 BREAK THE CLOISTER CODE

WATCH OUT!
THERE IS A WEEPING ANGEL
HIDING IN THE CLOISTERS.
DO NOT BLINK!

P. 29 CALLING ALL AGENTS!

P. 37 WHO SAID WHAT?

1. OHILA. 2. RASMUSSEN. 3. RIVER SONG.
4. THE DOCTOR. 5. BENNETT. 6. MISSY.

P. 56 TIME AND RELATIVE DIMENSION IN SEARCH

R U H X Q C E B C T W W N S K C U T C A L L S
H O O B T A I N A B L E K R J X E F E I A G X
U B F K P K E S A H W L L A H N G C C H V K K
L Q B E Z F N C X D R L K S O H N C X D P Q Y
M Y L H F J N X A A V B I H K A N N U U Z P Q
H V V L X E S U R R S I P T T I P O B F I Y Q
O Y K D U K S R R C S E C S F M P L G X W X I
H H I D Z P P E H P L L I E A Y I J U S K T Q
W O L F O D Q S T E P S K C L C V L R F R A Q
T P I D F O Y P T R S T I M M E D I A T E L Y
O K T E F N H O Y A B T B B E S C K J E E D Q
P G D C I E R N T L O X J N L W G I M X A F R
E Y O M C E Q D M P F Z M P J F E Y L L I B M
N H B L E R T O B J P N H E U R V J E O N H E
C Q Q N R F S H V O D J N L X K K K X P P M X
X D E K S E U U Z A Q Q G H Z W Y U J D F V L

P. 58-59 OI! WERE YOU PAYING ATTENTION?

MONSTERS
1: A (Water)
2: A (A split quantum actualiser)
3: C (It's venomous)

FRIENDS
1: A (Susan)
2: B (Homo Reptilia)
3: C (The Library)

PLANETS
1: B (I hid it in a pocket universe)
2: C (New Earth)
3: A (The Daleks)

ME
1: B (Twice)
2: C (Azbantium)
3: A (Davros)

TRUTH OR CONSEQUENCES
1: True
2: True
3: True
4: False
5: True

P. 60 FRIEND FROM THE FUTURE

B and F are identical.